Daniel Defoe was born in London, England in 1660.

Robinson Crusoe was first published in 1719, and remains one of his most popular novels.

This edition published in 1994 by SMITHMARK Publishers Inc., 16 East 32nd Street, New York, NY 10016.

SMITHMARK books are available for bulk purchase for sales promotion and premium use. For details write or call the manager of special sales, SMITHMARK Publishers Inc., 16 East 32nd Street, New York, NY 10016; (212) 532-6600.

Produced by Brompton Books Inc.
15 Sherwood Place
Greenwich, CT 06830

ISBN 0-8317-1665-7

Printed in Hong Kong

10 9 8 7 6 5 4 3 2 1

VAN GOOL'S

Robinson Crusoe

SMITHMARK

Chapter 1
ONE VOYAGE TOO MANY

Robinson Crusoe walked down to the beach, sat on a rock and opened his journal.
He began to write:

"Today is the 30th of September 1681. It is exactly twenty-two years since I landed on this island. I can hardly believe how long I have been here. For all this time I have been alone, except for a parrot which I have named Jack. If anyone were to see me now, they would never believe that I was once an elegant young Englishman, dressed in the height of fashion. Instead they would see a shaggy-haired, bearded savage clad in goatskins. They would also see that I am carrying a gun, for this morning I made a frightening discovery. I found the remains of a fire on the beach and in the embers were some bones. At first I was delighted to learn that someone had finally come to my island, but as I looked closer my delight turned to horror – they were human bones!
My visitors are cannibals!"

Not for the first time Robinson cursed himself for his foolishness all those years ago. He had lived with his family in York, a beautiful city in northern England. His father was keen to see him settled in a respectable profession, such as the law, but Robinson's ambitions lay in another direction. Since childhood he had dreamed of travelling the world, and often visited the docks at Hull to watch the great sailing ships. His parents were disappointed but, seeing that his heart was set on a career at sea, they reluctantly gave him their blessing. So on his nineteenth birthday he joined a ship sailing to London. The passage was rough, and he was ill for the whole journey, but he was not put off. He wrote home frequently, and one day mentioned to his father that when he had saved enough he was hoping to join a ship sailing for Guinea in Africa. His father, always the most generous of men, sent him the money he needed for his fare.

When Robinson returned from Africa, he brought back a small quantity of gold, which he sold in London for a handsome profit. "You've a good head for business, young Robinson!" remarked the ship's captain. But although it was pleasant to make money, it was the adventure Robinson loved, and within a few weeks he was preparing for another journey to Guinea. He stayed there for two years, then sailed to Brazil where he made friends with a young Portuguese lad. They bought a farm together and grew tobacco and sugar cane.

But after four years he became restless and longed to travel again. He booked a passage back to Guinea. "I will bring back ivory, gold and spices," he said to his partner. "With the money I make from selling them, we will be able to improve the farm." Then leaving the business in his partner's hands, he took to the ocean once more.

However, Robinson was not destined to reach Guinea. Just north of the Brazilian coast, a terrible storm blew up. The raging wind tore the sails to tatters and splintered the masts. Huge waves battered the ship and hurled it against the rocks. The crew made for the lifeboats, but they capsized as soon as they hit the water. Robinson grabbed a piece of wreckage and managed to stay afloat, but saw to his horror that he was the only survivor. He began to swim like a madman, only just keeping his head above the water.

Tossed about on the waves like a piece of driftwood, Robinson felt himself getting weaker and weaker. Finally, just when he thought he would surely die, an enormous wave washed him up onto a sandy beach. Exhausted, he lost consciousness.

When he awoke the sun was shining and the sea was calm. The splintered wreck of the ship had come to rest close to the shore. "Where am I?" wondered Robinson. He looked around but saw no other signs of life. Once he felt strong enough he swam over to the wreck to explore. He had hoped to find some food, and maybe some fresh water, but to his delight the wreck proved to be a treasure trove! Not only did he find food and water, but a variety of tools: knives, a hammer, rope and a pickaxe.

Robinson bundled everything into some empty corn sacks. He gathered wood from the wreck and tied it together with heavy rope to make a clumsy raft. Then he carried his provisions back to the beach.

On his second trip he took back some rifles, together with a bible, a telescope and paper and ink that he had found in the poor captain's cabin. It was lucky he visited the wreck when he did, for a few days later another storm blew up, and the wreck was sunk completely.

Chapter 2
ROBINSON BUILDS A HOME

That first night Robinson slept on the beach, but he was nervous out in the open, and knew he had to make some kind of shelter. He chose a spot at the foot of a cliff, close to a spring of fresh water.

Hauling branches from the forest he built two stout fences to form a stockade around the cliff. The only way in or out was by a ladder, which Robinson kept inside the stockade at night. Now he could sleep securely!

As soon as the fences were finished he set to work building a cabin to live in. His new home took many days to build, but at last he stood back to admire his work. It was rough, but strong, and he felt very pleased with himself.

At the very bottom of the cliff was a narrow cave, where Robinson stored all the supplies he'd taken from the ship. He knew that his food would not last long, so as soon as his shelter was finished he went hunting. To his delight he found plenty of wild animals and birds on the island.

Once he had made sure that he would not starve, Robinson began to furnish his new home. Trying to remember the craftsmen he had seen when he was a child, he made a table, chairs and a bed.

While exploring the other side of the island, he discovered an area of thick, muddy clay. After a few attempts he was able to make rough plates and bowls, leaving them to dry out in the sun.

So that he would have light in the evenings he made lamps from coconut oil. The smell was disgusting, but he was very proud of his ingenuity. In those early days he was so busy and had so much to learn about his island that he was almost content.

One day he caught two goats, and made a wooden pen for them close to his cabin. Every year his little herd got bigger, and he had fresh meat and milk whenever he needed it. Some time later, he was surprised to discover a small patch of corn growing near the beach. At first he was puzzled, but then remembered the corn sacks he had brought from the ship. He had thought they were empty, but a few grains must have been caught inside and fallen to the ground. Thanks to the sun and the tropical rains his little cornfield thrived.

But although his life on the island was pleasant, he never gave up hope of being rescued.

"21st December 1681. In my last entry I wrote about finding the remains of the cannibals' horrible feast. Well, today I have seen the cannibals themselves! This morning, as I was hunting in the forest, I noticed smoke coming from the beach. I kept well hidden in the trees and crept forward to take a look. There were two canoes pulled up on the beach, and farther up the shore were nine cannibals feasting around a fire. 'They must have come here to celebrate a victory,' I thought. After the cannibals left I could not bring myself to examine the fire, but let the tide carry away the grisly remains.

This is a cruel, wild country.

Ever since my arrival on the island, I have been praying for rescue, but since seeing the cannibals I have been even more desperate to escape. The other day I thought my prayers had been answered. There had been a storm during the night, but by morning it was calm. As I walked down the beach, I stopped in astonishment. 'Look, Jack!' I cried. 'A ship!' I waved my arms and cried aloud, then suddenly remembered the storm. Sure enough, when I looked through my telescope and saw the broken masts and tattered sails, I realised the terrible truth – the ship was a wreck. I searched the sea for hours, but saw no sign of any survivors. That afternoon I went to explore the new wreck, which was a Spanish galleon. Suddenly I saw that there had been a survivor after all – a dog! He was so pleased to see me that he jumped into the water and swam to meet me."

Here Robinson Crusoe closed his journal for the night.

Chapter 3
FRIDAY STEPS OUT OF A DREAM

After the visits by the cannibals and the wreck of the galleon, Robinson felt sure that another ship would pass his island. But three long years went by before he saw another human being. He became so lonely and desperate for company, that one night he had a vivid dream. He dreamed that cannibals came to the island again, this time bringing a prisoner. Just as they were about to kill him, the prisoner escaped and fled into the forest. Here Robinson found him, and hid him in the cabin until the cannibals left. At last he had a friend! That morning, Robinson wrote in his journal:

"I was so happy when I awoke, for I believed it had really happened and I had a companion at last. I was heartbroken to discover it was only a dream."

Some days later, more canoes landed on the island, and the cannibals brought a prisoner with them. From his cabin Robinson watched the scene through his telescope. Suddenly he exclaimed, "My goodness! Am I still dreaming?" For the prisoner suddenly slipped away, and ran into the forest as fast as his legs would carry him. Two of the cannibals came after him.

Robinson waited until they were out of sight of their companions. Then taking a gun he crept down to the beach, followed the first cannibal and shot him dead. The second cannibal was so terrified by the gunshot that he dropped his bow and arrows and ran back to the canoes, shrieking in fright.

The cannibals' prisoner stood before Robinson, trembling from head to foot. He seemed just as scared of his rescuer as he had been of his captors. Robinson put his gun down, and tried to signal to the terrified man that he was friendly. He beckoned him closer, saying, "I will not hurt you."

The young native watched him closely, then seemed to decide that Robinson meant him no harm. He threw himself to the ground before Robinson, then gestured wildly at the dead cannibal lying a few feet away.

Eventually Robinson realised that the young man was thanking him for saving his life. Then the native began to speak in a strange language. "I don't understand you," said Robinson, sadly. But it was still good to hear a human voice for the first time in over twenty-five years.

Robinson led the man to his cabin, and gave him bread and milk. While his new friend was eating, he returned to watch the cannibals on the beach. They had leapt into their canoes, and were rowing away as fast as they could.

"It's just like my dream!" thought Robinson as he walked back to his cabin.

"You need a name, my lad," he said, then laughed aloud. "Well, today is Friday, so to mark the day I found a friend, that is what I shall call you!" Friday grinned back, and began to make signs. When he realised what the young man was trying to ask him, Robinson wondered what he had let himself in for! Friday was suggesting that to celebrate his escape they should eat the two savages they'd killed!

"I'll have to cure you of these horrible habits," said Robinson, shaking his head.

Robinson prepared a place for Friday to sleep. He was a little concerned about sharing his home with a cannibal, and hung up a hammock between the two fences. "It would be foolish to trust him too quickly," he thought. "He may attack me in my sleep!" But he need not have worried, for Friday was always friendly and eager to learn.

The only disagreement they had was about clothes. Friday didn't like wearing them, and Robinson insisted that he should. "Where I come from, Friday, it is not polite to go around naked!" Eventually Friday grew used to wearing the clothes that Robinson made for him. And after a while he even became quite proud of them!

Chapter 4
THE SPANISH GALLEON

The next few months were happy ones.
Robinson was delighted to have a close friend
once more. He taught Friday to look after the
goats and to milk them, and how to tend the
corn. Friday was curious about everything
and learnt quickly.

Often as he watched Friday, Robinson
would think, "I am old enough to be his
father," and soon Friday was like the son he
had never had. Within a year the young
native could speak and understand English
quite well.

Robinson learned from Friday too. One
evening, Friday took him to the top of the
cliffs, and pointing all around him he
exclaimed, "Benamuckee made all this!"

"Is Benamuckee your god?" asked
Robinson and Friday nodded. "Well, then I
thank him for sending you to me," said
Robinson with a smile.

Often as they cooked their evening meal, Friday would tell Robinson about his life. "Many tribes live on the islands near here," he explained. "Most of them are peaceful, but some are always fighting. The men you rescued me from are the most fearsome tribe of all."

"Are there any men with pale skin like mine?" asked Robinson. "There are white men living far away on the mainland in the West," replied Friday. "But they never come to the islands."

Robinson was disappointed until Friday added, "But when I was younger, a group of white men came to my island in a lifeboat, almost dead from hunger. Their ship had been wrecked and my people looked after them. They were still there when I was captured." Perhaps these were survivors from the wreck of the Spanish galleon.

One day Friday came running up from the beach in terror. "Look! Three canoes!" Robinson quickly loaded a couple of guns, and the friends began to make their way down to the beach. Twenty natives were gathered around two prisoners who stood with their arms tied behind their backs. One was pale skinned. Robinson was sure that he must be one of the Spanish sailors Friday had described to him.

"Come on, Friday. We must save these men!" he whispered. They took aim at the cannibals and began to shoot, killing two of them. The others looked around fearfully. Robinson and Friday reloaded, and killed four more. "That's frightened them!" said Robinson. "Now follow me." At the sight of the strangers running out of the forest with guns blazing, the group fled.

Robinson untied the Spaniard. "Quick, take this gun and help us!" he cried. Soon the last cannibals ran for their canoes, and rowed frantically away.

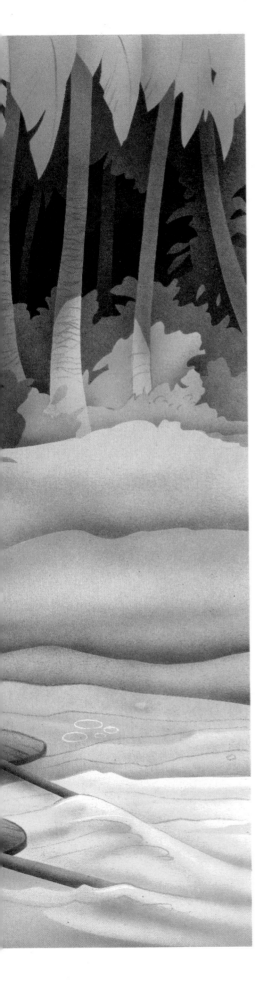

When Friday saw the second prisoner, he was overcome with emotion! "It is . . . my father!" he said, in tears. The two men hugged. But there was another surprise. When the dog saw the Spaniard, he leapt and barked in excitement. The man really was a survivor from the wrecked galleon.

"Sixteen of us managed to get away during the storm," he said.

"You must go back to them," said Robinson. "See if you can persuade your friends to join us here. It will be safer if we are all together. This island has everything we need." So a few days later, Friday's father and the Spaniard set out to sea once more, hoping to return with the others.

Chapter 5
ROBINSON FIGHTS THE PIRATES

Before a week had passed, Robinson found himself looking out to sea. He knew it would take the others longer to return, but he was very impatient. One morning he could hardly believe his eyes. "There's something on the horizon!" he cried. Quickly he raised his telescope, and gasped in amazement. It was not a group of canoes, but a sailing ship, and an English one at that! "After all this time!" cried Robinson. He watched as a boat was lowered from the vessel, and was rowed towards the island. As she got closer, Robinson counted eleven men on board. "Three of them are tied up," he said, puzzled. "I wonder why?"

"Do the English eat their prisoners too?" exclaimed Friday, almost hopefully. "Certainly not!" replied Robinson, spluttering with laughter. But what were these sailors doing?

A group of them set off to explore the island. They had left two men to guard their prisoners. But they soon fell asleep.

"Come on Friday. Let's see what's going on," whispered Robinson. "We'll tie up that lazy pair, and release their prisoners!" The two men crept along the sand, and the sleeping sailors hardly had time to struggle before they found themselves securely bound.

"I'm the captain of that ship," said the eldest prisoner. He explained that three crewmen had started a mutiny. "They wanted to be pirates. They didn't dare kill me, but they planned to leave me here, with my two faithful lieutenants. The rest of the crew were too scared to stop them."

Just then there were gunshots, and the other eight pirates came running down the beach. Robinson and Friday shot back, and two were killed. The others threw down their weapons and surrendered. "The rest of the crew are bound to wonder what's happened to their mates," said Robinson. "We'd better get out of sight." After tying the captives' hands behind their backs, Robinson led the way back to the stockade.

A little while later another boat landed on the beach, this time with ten men on board. "There's Atkins!" exclaimed the captain. "He's the ringleader."

Suddenly one of the captured mutineers called out from inside the cabin, "Captain, I'm sorry I joined the mutiny. Please let me help you fight Atkins!" The captain stared at him for a moment, then said, "I trust you, Will Frye. You're not a bad lad."

"We'll help you too, Captain," called the others. "Please give us another chance." Robinson and the captain untied the men, and gave each of them a gun.

"Here's my plan," explained Robinson. "We're going to trick them into believing we've got a whole army here. With any luck they'll surrender without a fight." They watched the pirates creeping warily up the beach. Then Robinson nodded at Will, who cried out, "Is that you Atkins? You'd better surrender. There's a whole English regiment here. You can't escape!"

Terrified, Atkins and his men threw down their guns at once. Robinson's trick had worked and without a shot being fired! The captain and his men marched the pirates back to the cabin at gunpoint.

Robinson dressed himself in one of the lieutenant's uniforms, and had the ten mutineers brought before him. "I am the governor of this island," he declared sternly. "You are all under arrest."

Then he turned to the captain. "Are there any men still on board?" he asked. "Yes," replied the captain. "But they shouldn't give us any trouble. Most of them only went along with the mutiny because they were scared of Atkins. He filled their heads with all sorts of foolish ideas. But you've learned your lesson now, lads, haven't you?" The men who'd come ashore with Atkins looked very ashamed.

"Do any of you lads want to help me take the ship back?" the captain asked the shame-faced pirates. Eager to make up for their foolishness all but three joined the captain as he headed back to the ship. A few shots were fired, but soon the captain was in control again. "I owe you my life," he told Robinson.

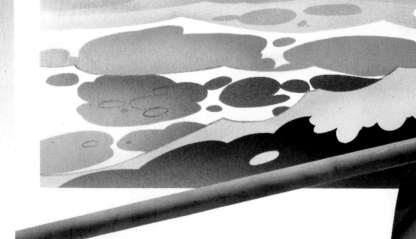

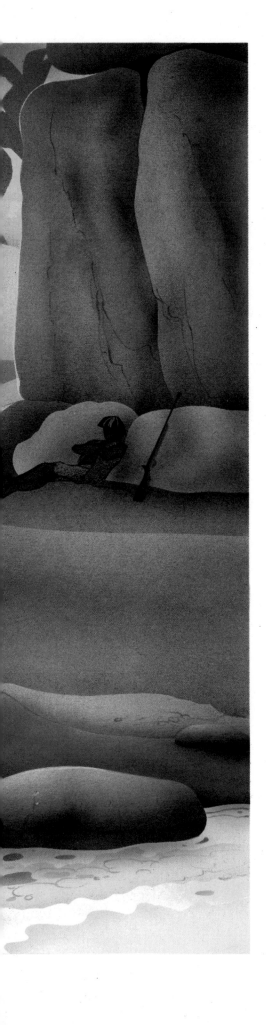

By nightfall, Robinson's island was peaceful once more. The three prisoners were firmly bound, and guards were taking it in turns to watch them. Everyone was sleeping except for Robinson himself. He sat on the beach, his head in a whirl. "After twenty-eight years, two months and nineteen days, I'm going home! I can hardly believe I'm not dreaming!" Eventually tiredness overcame him, and he fell asleep on the sand.

The next morning the captain shook him awake. "The mutiny has wasted a lot of time," he said, "I must set sail immediately. Are you ready to leave?" Quickly Robinson gathered a few possessions and, after taking a last look around the island, he and Friday followed the captain onto the ship.

"What are you planning to do with Atkins and his gang?" asked Robinson. "I did want to take them back to England for trial, but they have begged me to let them stay here."

Chapter 6
HOMECOMING

Robinson's journal continued:

"It was a fine day in June 1687 when our ship reached the docks in London. Friday and I said our goodbyes to the captain and set off for York, where my sister still lived. 'We thought you were dead!' she cried, through her tears. 'We had a letter from Brazil, to say that your ship had been lost.' That evening I wrote to my Portuguese friend, telling him that I was alive and well. This was my reply, 'Dear Robinson, I cannot tell you how happy I am that you are alive! And I have some good news for you too – you are rich! Our farm has done well, and half belongs to you. I will send the money to England at once.'

But what do you think happened to me next? Although by then I was over fifty, I fell in love and was married! I used my new-found wealth wisely and bought a large farm in the English countryside, where I lived with my dear wife. My brother had died while I was away and his two sons came to live with us.

Over the years my wife and I had two sons of our own, and a beautiful little daughter. My family were fascinated by my adventures, and often in the evenings they would beg Friday and I to tell them stories about the island. My youngest nephew was so enthralled by these tales that he vowed to go to sea himself. And now, several years later, he is captain of his own ship, and I am very proud of him.

But my dear wife is not here to share my happiness, for last year she fell ill, and did not recover. I missed her dreadfully, so on the 8th of January 1695 I decided to book a passage on my nephew's ship and visit my island once more. My faithful friend Friday came with me on the voyage.

On the island, several surprises were in store for us. Where my modest cabin once stood, a village of twenty wooden huts had sprung up. For Friday's father and the Spaniards had returned! The old man told me that there was a village on the south of the island too. "What became of the three English criminals?" I asked. "They've settled down!" said the old man with a smile. "They live in the other village, and all three have families!"

One day I decided to explore some of the neighbouring islands. Friday came with me, and I wish he had not, for a terrible tragedy occurred. As we approached the nearest island, we suddenly found ourselves under attack from the natives. Arrows filled the air and, to my horror, poor Friday was hit. The wound was deep, and he died in my arms.

What was I to do now? I could not face returning to England straight away, so in a fit of madness I decided to do what I had always dreamed of – travel the world. I visited the Cape of Good Hope, Madagascar, Arabia, and the ports of India. I celebrated my sixty-ninth birthday in Thailand. From there I travelled to China, spending time in the forbidden city of Peking. Finally I crossed the desolate mountains and plains of Siberia on horseback. At last I felt ready to return home. And here I'll stay.

I am now a very old man, and my wandering days are over. But I have some incredible memories. And every evening my young grandsons beg me to tell them their favourite story – my adventures on the island."